THE MAGIC of Ooh La La

by Fangfei Li
illustrated by Xiaoxian Dong

Reycraft Books
55 FIfth Avenue
New York, NY 10003

Reycraftbooks.com

Reycraft Books is a trade imprint and trademark of Newmark Learning, LLC.

This edition is published by arrangement with China Children's Press & Publication Group, China.
© China Children's Press & Publication Group

All rights reserved. No portion of this book may be reproduced, stored in a retrieval system, or transmitted in any form or by any means, electronic, mechanical, photocopying, recording, or otherwise, without written permission from the publisher. For information regarding permission, please contact info@reycraftbooks.com.

Educators and Librarians: Our books may be purchased in bulk for promotional, educational, or business use. Please contact sales@reycraftbooks.com.

This is a work of fiction. Names, characters, places, dialogue, and incidents described either are the product of the author's imagination or are used fictitiously. Any resemblance to actual persons, living or dead, is entirely coincidental.

Sale of this book without a front cover or jacket may be unauthorized. If this book is coverless, it may have been reported to the publisher as "unsold or destroyed" and may have deprived the author and publisher of payment. Library of Congress Cataloging-in-Publication Data is available.

ISBN: 978-1-4788-6878-1
Printed in Guangzhou, China
4401/0919/CA21901491
10 9 8 7 6 5 4 3 2 1
First Edition Paperback published by Reycraft Books 2019

Reycraft Books and Newmark Learning, LLC, support diversity and the First Amendment, and celebrate the right to read.

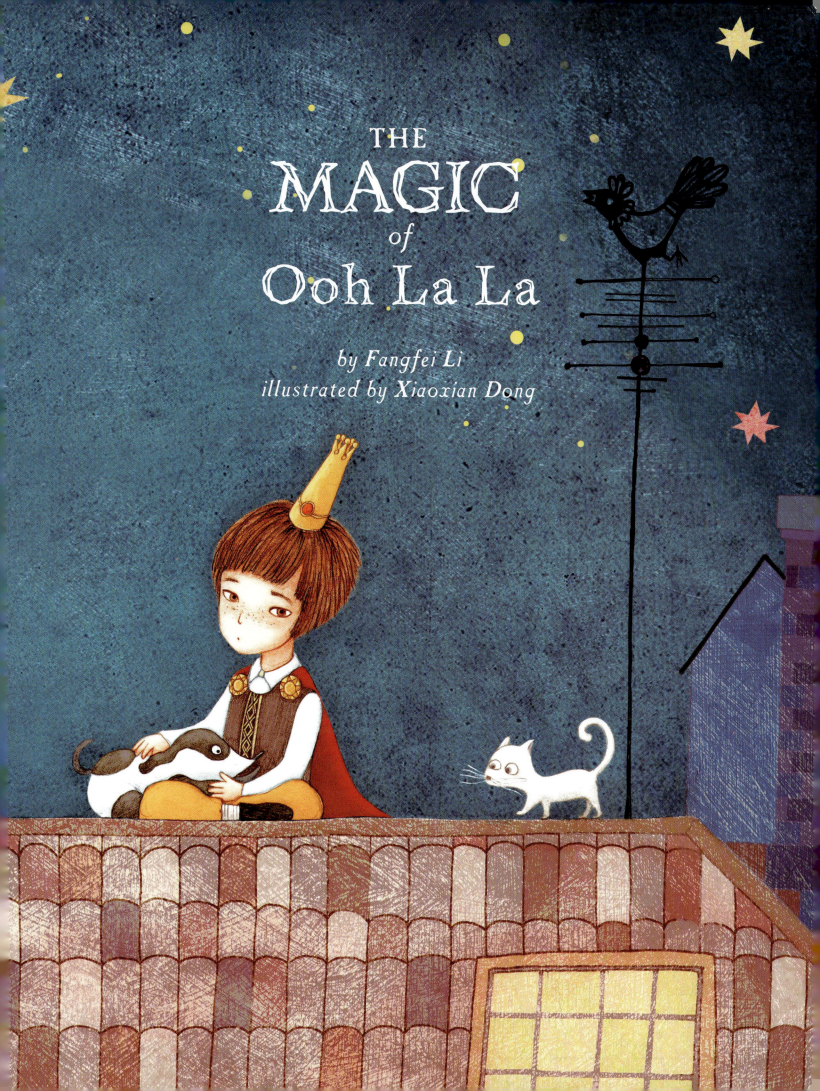

Far away, high in the clouds, lies the magical kingdom of Ooh La La. Those who live in Ooh La La have the power to create whatever they want—just by imagining it.

The people of Ooh La La might want valuable jewels, or fancy feasts, or magnificent palaces. And PRESTO! If they can imagine it, they can have it.

But once there was a boy who never felt happy in Ooh La La. He didn't like imagining treasures or palaces that came to life. Instead, he spent most of his time gazing down at Earth, wishing he could visit. He wondered if on Earth, perhaps, he might find happiness.

On the boy's eighth birthday, the King of Ooh La La finally granted his wish. The boy could visit Earth for three days, during which he could try to find happiness. But there was one rule—the boy couldn't use his powers on Earth.

As soon as he got to Earth, the boy realized it might be difficult to find happiness without using his powers. Everything on Earth cost money. And the boy didn't have any.

So on his first day, the boy found a job in a restaurant. He washed piles and piles of dishes, from early in the morning until late at night. Afterwards, the King of Ooh La La said, "My child, you certainly didn't find happiness on Earth today. Only hard work and water-shriveled fingers. You seemed happier in Ooh La La."

The boy knew the King was right.

On his second day, the boy tried another job. He worked as a messenger and delivered packages from early in the morning until late at night. Afterwards, he was too tired to even eat dinner.

He had not found happiness. And he had only one day left on Earth.

That night, the boy looked up into the stars, toward his home in Ooh La La. Was the King right? Was he happier when he could create everything with his imagination?

Somehow, the boy felt there had to be more.

On his third and last day on Earth, the boy discovered a big, green garden. It had winding stone paths, and trees and bushes with extraordinary shapes. He had never seen anything like it. It was . . . magical! But it was a different kind of magical than what he knew on Ooh La La.

Every garden in Ooh La La was created with someone's imagination. But this garden had been created with someone's hands. Someone had planted all the trees and flowers. Someone's hands had nurtured them and helped them grow.

The boy found the man who created the garden and asked to be his helper.

The boy learned much from the gardener. He learned how to plant seeds, clip bushes, pull weeds, water plants, and trim trees. It was the happiest day the boy could ever remember.

As the sun set, the gardener showed the boy how to make a delicious dinner from things in the garden. He picked fresh vegetables, collected eggs from his hens, and made a sweet pudding from his pear tree. The boy thought it was the best dinner he had ever eaten.

Soon it was time to say farewell. The gardener gave the boy a red bag as payment for all his hard work.

When the boy opened the red bag the gardener had given him, he saw that it contained a packet filled with all sorts of seeds.

The boy journeyed back to Ooh La La and went to see the King. "I found happiness on Earth!" said the boy. "But it wasn't Earth that made me happy. It was making something magical with my own hands and my own hard work."

The King smiled. "Congratulations, my dear child. You found something you love and THAT is something you can take with you wherever you go for the rest of your life."

So the boy decided to use his hands, his hard work, and his heart. He planted flowers and trees all over Ooh La La, using what he learned from the gardener.

The people loved watching the magical process of a seed taking root and growing into something beautiful. And the boy was truly happy. At last.